The Hee-Haw River

DEE LILLEGARD • Illustrated by ALLAN EITZEN

HENRY HOLT AND COMPANY   NEW YORK

Henry Holt and Company, Inc.
Publishers since 1866
115 West 18th Street
New York, New York 10011

Henry Holt is a registered
trademark of Henry Holt and Company, Inc.

Published in Canada by Fitzhenry & Whiteside Ltd.,
195 Allstate Parkway, Markham, Ontario L3R 4T8.

Library of Congress Cataloging-in-Publication Data
Lillegard, Dee.
The hee-haw river / Dee Lillegard; illustrated by Allan Eitzen.
Summary: Annoyed when the farmer's wife complains about its
murmur, the river sets in motion a confusing chain of events
by stealing the mule's hee-haw.
[1. Rivers—Fiction. 2. Animal sounds—Fiction.
3. Sound—Fiction. I. Eitzen, Allan, ill. II. Title
PZ7.L6275He 1995 [E]—dc20   94-20305

ISBN 0-8050-2375-5

First Edition—1995

Printed in the United States of America
on acid-free paper. ∞
1   3   5   7   9   10   8   6   4   2

For Wayne

— *D . L .*

For my grandsons, Dietrich and Erich

— *A . E .*

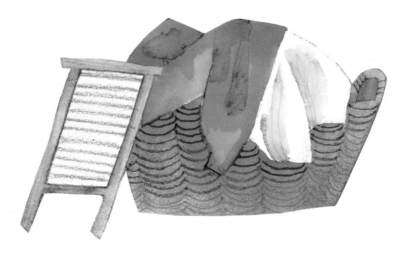

One hot summer day, Farmer Bean's wife knelt by the river with her big old scrub board and a week's wash.

"Work, work, work . . ." she grumbled. "And never any excitement."

The river that ran slowly through the middle of the farm was murmuring low, which annoyed Mrs. Bean.

"You lazy old river!" she said. "All you can do is murmur. You're so slow, I wonder you don't just stop."

At that, the river *did* stop! It lay in the middle of the farm, still as a stone.

"Oh, dear," cried Mrs. Bean. "What have I done? Run, you lazy old river! Run!"

But the river lay in the middle of the farm and wouldn't move an inch. It was tired of running and murmuring, and tired of hearing the farmer's wife complain.

"You're not only lazy, you're stubborn," said Mrs. Bean. *"Stubborn as a mule!"*

Then, "Drat!" she muttered to herself. "I've forgotten my soap. I must go back to the house and fetch it."

Oh, the sun was oven hot, and the whole
farm was baking. The farmer's mule, and his
cow, and his pig came to the river's edge to
cool off.

"Mooo . . ." said the cow. "It's *tooo hot!*"

"Oink!" said the pig. "I need a drink!"

"Me, too," said the mule. "*Hee-Haw!*" Then he stuck his head into the river . . . and *that* is when the mischievous river stole the mule's *hee-haw*.

Oh, that river was happy to be doing something different! The farmer's wife had said it was like a mule—why shouldn't it *sound* like one?

"Hee-haw! Hee-haw!" went the river.

The mule opened his mouth to reply, but not a sound came out. He looked at the cow mooing. And all at once, he ran in front of the cow, opening his mouth wide as if he were taking a bite out of the air.

"MOO! MOO!" went the mule.

The cow opened her mouth to reply, but not a sound came out. She looked at the pig oinking. And all at once, she ran in front of the pig and opened her mouth wide as if she were yawning.

"OINK! OINK!" went the cow.

When the pig found herself without an *oink*, she decided to steal the cat's *meow*. She ran in front of the cat, opening her mouth wide as if she would chomp on a corncob. But instead...

"MEOW! MEOW!" went the pig.

Now the cat was on his way to Farmer Bean's house to have a slurp of milk. When he opened his mouth to *meow*, nothing came out. So he decided to steal the buzz of a bee who happened to be zipping by.

"BZZZ, BZZZ" went the cat as he scratched at the kitchen door.

"It's a funny kind of bee that can scratch at my door," said Farmer Bean's wife. She would not open the door because she was afraid to be stung. So the cat could not get in for his slurp of milk.

Now the cat decided that he would rather have his own *meow* than be buzzing around like the bee. Suddenly he was angry. He blamed the pig for stealing his *meow*.

Then the pig blamed the cow for stealing her *oink*.

The cow blamed the mule for stealing her *moo*.

And the mule blamed the river that wouldn't run for stealing his *hee-haw*.

"**MOOO!** Make that river *moove!*" said the
mule to Farmer Bean, who was working
in the barn.

Farmer Bean scratched his balding head and wondered what the noise was all about. Then he decided it was time to go fishing. He packed up his gear to take down to the river.

"Hee-haw! Hee-haw!" went the river.

"Such a commotion!" said the farmer.

Since there was no more buzzing and scratching at her door, Mrs. Bean decided to go down to the river to scrub the farmer's clothes. She carried her soap past the cow, and the pig, and the hungry cat. She hurried past her husband, who was loping along with his fishing pole. Then she knelt at the edge of the river that would not run.

"You stubborn old river . . ." she started to say.

But before she could finish, the river replied with a great "Hee-haw! Hee-haw!"

"Help!" cried Farmer Bean's wife. "The mule is drowning in the river!"

She jumped into the river with all her clothes on and thrashed about, trying to save the mule.

"Hee-haw! Hee-haw!" went the river.

"I've got you!" cried the farmer's wife, as she grabbed the branch of a tree, thinking it was the mule's tail.

When Farmer Bean heard the hubbub, he dropped his fishing pole and came running to the river, thinking that Mrs. Bean was drowning. He jumped in and thrashed about, trying to save her.

"I've got you!" cried Farmer Bean, grabbing his wife's shoes and pulling them off.

Now the mule, hearing all the noise, came running to the river, thinking that Farmer Bean and his wife were drowning. "MOO!" he cried. Then he jumped in with a big splash and sank his teeth into Farmer Bean's behind, trying to save him.

All this commotion was more than the river could stand. It began to run away. It ran faster and faster, with a *rush-rush* sound, leaving the mule's *hee-haw*, and everything else, behind it.

One by one, the animals and the farmer and his wife came dripping out of the water, all tuckered out.

Farmer Bean's wife took one look at the soaking mule. "Thank goodness, I saved you!" she said.

"Hee-Haw!" went the mule.

"Mooo!" went the cow.

"Oink! Oink!" went the pig.

"Meow! Meow!" went the cat, all wet and bedraggled.

Now the farmer's wife noticed that the river
was rushing away.

"Rush, rush, rush . . ." she muttered.
"What's the big hurry?"

Farmer Bean stood scratching his balding
head.

"As for you," said Mrs. Bean, scowling at her dripping-wet husband, "if you like the water so much, wash your own clothes!"

Then she tossed the soap at Farmer Bean, and trotted back to her kitchen to have a nice cup of tea.